ALY & AJ'S ROCK 'N' ROLL MYSTERIES

FIRST STOP, NEW YORK

by Tracey West and Katherine Noll
illustrated by Aly Michalka

GROSSET & DUNLAP
Published by the Penguin Group
Penguin Group (USA) Inc., 375 Hudson Street, New York, New York 10014, USA
Penguin Group (Canada), 90 Eglinton Avenue East, Suite 700, Toronto, Ontario M4P 2Y3,
Canada (a division of Pearson Penguin Canada Inc.)
Penguin Books Ltd., 80 Strand, London WC2R 0RL, England
Penguin Group Ireland, 25 St. Stephen's Green, Dublin 2, Ireland
(a division of Penguin Books Ltd.)
Penguin Group (Australia), 250 Camberwell Road, Camberwell, Victoria 3124, Australia
(a division of Pearson Australia Group Pty. Ltd.)
Penguin Books India Pvt. Ltd., 11 Community Centre, Panchsheel Park,
New Delhi—110 017, India
Penguin Group (NZ), 67 Apollo Drive, Rosedale, North Shore 0632, New Zealand
(a division of Pearson New Zealand Ltd.)
Penguin Books (South Africa) (Pty.) Ltd., 24 Sturdee Avenue,
Rosebank, Johannesburg 2196, South Africa

Penguin Books Ltd., Registered Offices: 80 Strand, London WC2R 0RL, England

Cover photo courtesy of Joe Magnani.

Library of Congress Cataloging-in-Publication Data is available.

ISBN 978-0-448-44842-8   10 9 8 7 6 5 4 3 2 1

CHAPTER ONE:
MANIC MONDAY

"We got along, we got along, we got along until you did that. Now all I want is just my stuff back. Do you get that?"

The words to "Potential Breakup Song" drifted out of a hotel window onto the busy city street below. Up in the room, Aly and AJ sat cross-legged on the hotel room beds, strumming their acoustic guitars. The song had a whole different feel this way, played without electric guitars or keyboards, but the funky beat was still the same. The sisters sang together until AJ stopped playing.

"I think it's a good choice," she said.

Aly put her guitar on her lap and brushed a long strand of blond hair over her shoulder. "Are you sure?" she asked. "I mean, this is our opening song, on the opening night of our biggest tour yet. We need a really strong start."

"It *is* strong," AJ assured her. "It's a hot song. You know it."

Aly nodded. "You're right! I'm just a tiny bit nervous, I guess. It's Madison Square Garden, you know? We'll be performing in front of thousands of people."

AJ grinned. "Yeah, like, we've never done that before."

"You know what I mean," Aly said, flopping back on the bed. For the first time, she noticed the ceiling of the hotel room, which was painted with cupids floating on fluffy clouds.

"Wow. Some ceiling," Aly said.

AJ leaned back, too. "Not bad," she said. She glanced around the room. It was fancier than most hotel rooms, but otherwise, it was a lot like every hotel room they'd ever seen: two beds, side by side; a small table with two chairs; and a dresser with a television set on top of it. This room also had a small sitting area, with a red sofa covered in velvety fabric. "The only thing this room is missing is Hello Kitty. I miss our bus."

Every inch of Aly and AJ's tour bus was decorated with images of the adorable Japanese kitten. The bus had taken them all over the country, but they were going to be in Manhattan for almost a week, so their mom had arranged for hotel rooms for the entire crew.

"Me too," Aly said. "But hotel rooms have one thing that the bus doesn't." She reached over to the small table next to the bed and picked up a binder with a leather cover.

"Room service!" AJ said. "Great idea. I'm so hungry!"

She bounced over to Aly's bed and looked at the menu over her shoulder.

"Mmmm, pasta," AJ said.

"And cheeseburgers, with extra large onion rings," Aly added. "That sounds so good! Let's order right now."

She reached for the phone, but a knock on the door made her pause.

"Girls, are you ready?"

AJ ran to the door and opened it. The girls' mom, Carrie, stepped in. She had the same blond hair and bright smile as her daughters.

"Hey, Mom," AJ said.

"Hey, sweetie," Carrie said. "Are you girls ready? It's time to go."

"Go where?" Aly asked.

"You're special guests at the opening of the Girls Rock Academy, remember?" Carrie asked.

Aly jumped up. "Oh, cool! I remember now. That's the new guitar school for girls, right?"

"Right," Carrie said, looking at her watch. "But you've got to be there in twenty minutes."

"Definitely not cool," Aly replied. "But don't worry. We'll be ready in a minute."

Carrie nodded. "I'll meet you in the lobby."

"I can't believe we forgot," Aly said, shaking her head. "Should we bring Artemis and Jonah?" She nodded toward the guitars on the beds.

"I don't think we'll need them," AJ said. "I think we're just supposed to talk to the students of the school for a few minutes."

Aly began rummaging through a pile of clothes on the floor. She plucked out a short-sleeved black top; tiny hearts were cut into the sleeves. Aly held up the shirt in front of her. "What do you think? Does it scream 'guitar'?"

"Love it," AJ replied. "But change the belt. Maybe the one with the silver loops." She was opening a drawer in the carved wood dresser where she had neatly folded and placed all of her clothes. She pulled out a dusty brown peasant top with flowers stitched around the scoop neck. Her older sister nodded in approval.

"Now that screams 'acoustic guitar.' Very sixties," she said. "Wear the suede boots and it'll be the perfect outfit."

AJ shut the drawer. "We'd better hurry."

A few minutes later they rushed out of the elevator into the hotel lobby. Their mom stood by the open door of the hotel, a look of urgency on her face.

"I've hailed you a cab," she told them. "You've got to be at the school in fifteen minutes. I've got a meeting with a photographer, but I'll catch up with you later. Have fun!"

Each girl gave Carrie a quick kiss and scrambled inside the cab. The cab driver, a grandfatherly man with a gray mustache, smiled at them in the rearview mirror.

"My granddaughter Sarah loves you two," he said. "You make beautiful music. Don't worry, I'll get you to your gig in time."

"Thanks!" the girls said together.

They waved good-bye to Carrie as the cab screeched

away from the curb with a jolt. The name on the cab driver's license read MURRAY. Murray looked like a mild-mannered grandpa, but he drove like a NASCAR racer down Broadway.

The girls looked out the window at the crowds of people hurrying down the street carrying shopping bags and briefcases. It wasn't quite summer yet, but the spring day was warm and sunny—although the sun had to make its way past impossibly tall skyscrapers that cast shadows on the street below.

A car honked its horn angrily as Murray streaked past, cutting into the right lane. Aly and AJ gripped the seat backs in front of them as the cab hurtled around the corner. Aly couldn't help noticing the cute dresses in the clothing store as they raced past.

"I hope we have time to do some shopping this week," she said.

"I hope we make it through the week!" AJ joked, gripping her seat.

The cab jerked to a stop.

"Red light," Murray said. "And I was making good time, too."

Aly was suddenly distracted by a delicious smell coming through the window. She turned to see a pretzel cart on the side of the street. A young guy in an army jacket was working the cart.

"That smells sooooooo good," she said. She unrolled her window, then reached into her bag and took out a few dollars.

"Excuse me!" she called to the pretzel guy. "Two pretzels, please."

"With mustard!" AJ called behind her.

The pretzel guy didn't blink. He nodded, grabbed two hot pretzels from inside the cart, gave each one a quick squirt of mustard, and handed them to Aly in exchange for the cash.

"Thanks!" Aly said. The transaction happened just in time. Murray hit the gas again, and the cab lurched forward. Miraculously, there was no mustard disaster.

Aly and AJ bit into their pretzels.

"If New York City has a taste, then this might be it," Aly mused.

AJ nodded. "This is almost better than room service."

Murray drove on, and soon they saw a huge round building on the right.

"Madison Square Garden," Aly said, in almost a whisper.

"I can't believe we're playing there," AJ said. She took a deep breath. "Okay. Maybe now I'm a little nervous, too."

Below Madison Square Garden the streets seemed to get a little smaller and closer together. The buildings even got shorter. But there were just as many people, all in a hurry to get somewhere—just like Aly and AJ.

Luckily for them, Murray kept his promise. The cab jerked to a stop in front of a brownstone building on a tree-lined street.

"Fourteen minutes and twenty-eight seconds," Murray said, grinning. "I told you not to worry."

AJ paid for the cab ride, and handed Murray a business card.

"That's our tour manager, Jim," she said. "Give him a call and he'll make sure you and Sarah get tickets for the show."

Murray was thrilled. "You know, I've had celebrities in my cab before, but you girls are the best. As nice as they come. Sarah will be so happy."

Murray roared off, leaving a cloud of exhaust behind him. When the smoke cleared, the girls looked at the building. There were three brass plaques on the side of the glass door. One of the plaques read THE GIRLS ROCK ACADEMY.

"Guess this is the place," AJ said. "I thought this was some big grand opening. I wonder where everybody is."

At that moment, a distraught-looking young woman pushed through the front door. She wore jeans and a black T-shirt with a guitar and the letters *GRA*. Her white sneakers had a pattern of tiny black guitars, and a silver guitar-pick necklace completed her outfit. Her short black hair was spiked on top of her head, and her dark eyes were starting to fill with tears.

"The grand opening has been canceled!" she said, her voice choking. "The Girls Rock Academy is ruined!"

Gigi

CHAPTER TWO:
THE STOLEN GUITARS

Aly and AJ were too surprised to speak for a moment. Then Aly put an arm around the woman's shoulder.

"What happened?" AJ asked.

"Oh," the woman gasped, wiping the tears from her eyes. "Aly and AJ! I can't believe it's really you. I'm Gigi. Gigi Josephs, the owner of the school."

"Let's go inside and talk," AJ suggested. Gigi nodded and led them inside the brownstone building.

They walked down a narrow hallway and followed Gigi into a classroom. Folding chairs and music stands were scattered across the wood floor, but otherwise the room was pretty empty.

Gigi slumped into a chair. "I am so sorry. You two are, like, my idols, and it was so awesome of you to agree to come to the opening. And now there's nothing to open!"

"It's okay," Aly said. "Tell us what happened. Maybe we can help."

"This school is my dream. I've been playing guitar ever since I was seven years old. I listened to all the great women guitarists I could find, but there just aren't a lot out there," Gigi explained. "I knew there were more girls out there who want to learn how to rock out on guitar, just like us. That's why I opened this school."

"Wow!" AJ said. "That's a really great idea."

Aly smiled. "I would have loved to have gone to a school like this when I was a kid."

"But now everything is ruined," Gigi wailed. She

ran her fingers through her spiky hair. "Today was supposed to be the big day. I got here extra early this morning to make sure everything was perfect for the grand opening. But when I went to the equipment room, I discovered someone had broken in. They took electric guitars, amps, soundboards, everything!"

"That's awful!" Aly said sympathetically. "Did you call the police?"

Gigi shook her head. "Yes, but they said it won't be an easy case to solve. I need time to think. I sank all of my money into this place," she moaned. "Most schools are closed this week for spring break, and I signed up a bunch of girls for a week-long guitar camp. But I don't have a dime left to replace this equipment. How can I open a rock school without guitars or amps? All I've got left are a few acoustic guitars."

AJ looked around the room. "Where are the students?" she asked. "Isn't the grand opening supposed to start in a few minutes?"

"I called them all and told them there was a

power failure in the building. I needed to buy some time," Gigi explained. "I'm hoping the police might find the equipment soon and I'll be back in business. If the police don't track down the equipment soon, I'll have to return all the students' money—and close the school for good!"

"Gigi, that's horrible!" Aly said. "I feel so terrible for you."

"And for all those girls who won't be able to learn how to rock!" AJ added.

AJ and Aly looked at each other. They had one of those sister moments when they knew exactly what the other one was thinking. They both grinned, their eyes sparkling.

"I think we can help," AJ said. "Gigi, you can definitely reschedule the grand opening for tomorrow!"

"How?" Gigi asked. "I have no equipment!"

"Now you do," Aly said. "At least while we're in town. You can borrow all of our gear. We'll be in New York for a week. While we are here, it's yours."

"That will give you some time to try and get your stuff back," AJ said. "And in the meantime, the Girls Rock Academy will be open and jamming!"

"Oh!" Gigi gasped. "Are you sure? This is amazing!"

With a squeal of delight, Gigi hugged Aly first, then AJ.

"We'll be here tomorrow morning with our equipment," Aly said. "By tomorrow night, the Girls Rock Academy will be open for business!"

Gigi

CHAPTER THREE:
ANOTHER ROCK SCHOOL?

After accepting more hugs from a grateful Gigi, Aly and AJ stood on the sidewalk outside of the Girls Rock Academy.

"What rotten luck!" Aly said. "But I'm glad we're able to help."

"That's for sure," AJ said. "Boy, am I hungry. It seems like we ate those pretzels two days ago!"

"I'm hungry, too," Aly said. "But I don't think I'm up for another crazy cab ride around the city.

The weather is nice. Why don't we walk?"

"Sounds good," AJ agreed. "Maybe we can find a place to eat on the way."

"And maybe," Aly began, "we can—"

"—do some shopping!" AJ finished. "Sounds like the perfect day to me."

The girls took off down the street, comfortable among the tall buildings and crowded sidewalks. They'd spent part of their childhood in Seattle, Washington, and they liked the busy feel of a big city.

They were stopped at a crosswalk, waiting for the light to change, when a familiar tune caught their attention.

"Like it or love it or LEAVE it!"

"Hey! It's 'Like it or Leave it'!" Aly exclaimed.

It was a song from their album *Insomniatic*. The source of the music was a pickup truck. Three big, tough looking guys with tattoos were cranking Aly and AJ's music on the truck's sound system. One of the guys spotted them.

"Hey dudes—look! It's Aly and AJ!" he cried.

The guys in the truck looked at Aly and AJ with their mouths open. Then the driver threw the truck into park and stepped out—right in the middle of the street!

"I can't believe it. Girls, we gotta get your autographs," the driver said. Horns were honking all around, but he ignored them. "We've been listening to your album all day long on the job site. It keeps us going."

Aly and AJ signed autographs for all three men. They had brought traffic to a halt in the middle of New York City!

"Bye," said the driver, whose name was Dave. "We'll see you at Madison Square Garden!"

Aly and AJ couldn't stop laughing. They'd met all kinds of fans before, but none like this.

"That is one of the craziest things that's ever happened to us," Aly said. "Just wait until we tell Mom."

They were still laughing when they crossed the

street. Then AJ caught sight of a flyer posted on a lamppost on the corner. She stopped to read it.

"Aly, look at this," AJ said. "It's a poster for a rock school. The School for Girls Who Rock!"

"That's weird," Aly said. "Gigi just opened her girls' rock school a few blocks from here. This isn't a flyer for her school, is it?"

"I don't know," AJ said. "But look up ahead. It looks like someone is putting up more of these flyers. Let's find out."

A young woman was attaching more flyers to every lamppost and telephone pole on the street. She had on worn jeans with holes at the knees, a pair of lace-up boots, and an old concert T-shirt with a fitted blazer over it. Her long, straight black hair was parted in the center of her thin face. A pair of cat's-eye-shaped black glasses completed her look.

The girls walked up to her.

"Hey," Aly said in a friendly way. "Do you know Gigi from the Girls Rock Academy?"

The girl slowly stopped what she was doing and turned to face Aly and AJ. With a sneer on her face, she slowly looked them over from head to toe.

"Aren't you two supposed to be at the school opening?" she asked.

"It was postponed," Aly answered.

"Hmmm," she responded, arching an eyebrow. Then, without saying another word, she turned and walked off.

"Well, that was pretty rude!" AJ said. "What do you think that was all about?"

"I'm not sure," Aly said as she plucked one of the posters off a pole. "But we should take this with us. Obviously, whoever that girl was, she knew who we were—and knew we were supposed to be at the grand opening of the Girls Rock Academy."

AJ took the flyer from Aly. "Maybe it has something to do with the missing guitars," she said.

"What a long, strange day it's been!" Aly said. "And I know exactly what we need—some retail therapy."

Luckily, they happened to be standing in front of a fabulous shop that sold shoes and handbags. There were some awesome wedges, totally cool boots, and the latest flats displayed in the window.

"You know," Aly said, "we could really use some new shoes for our tour. They're practically a necessity."

They headed into the store and began oohing and aahing over the selection.

"Look at these," Aly held up a pair of classic Mary Janes with a twist—they had super long stiletto heels.

"Those are so cool," AJ said. "But we could break our necks on stage wearing something like that. What about these?" She held up a pair of brown buckled ankle boots.

"Now we're talking," Aly said as she grabbed a pair of Converse slip-ons with a design of pink and black checks. "I've never seen them in this color before."

But it was a pair of black knee-high boots that really grabbed their attention. The sleek and shiny boots zipped up and had a nice heel—tall, but not so tall that they'd have to worry about maneuvering safely on the stage.

"They will look great with that black skirt you have," AJ told Aly.

"And they'll look terrific with some skinny jeans, too," Aly said.

The girls left the shop with their packages and the glow of a successful shopping trip. It had grown dark while they were inside the shop and they passed a candy store, brightly lit inside. It seemed to be beckoning to Aly.

"I almost forgot how hungry I am," she said. "But now we can get something to eat!"

"Are you crazy?" AJ said. "You'll be bouncing off the walls and won't be able to sleep. Let's get some real food."

Aly sighed. "You're right. But the only other thing that will satisfy me right now is sushi!"

AJ grinned. "You're on."

They only had to walk a few more blocks until they spotted the perfect place: Sushi Island. The beautiful restaurant had a koi pond with a waterfall all around the dining area. They had to cross a little bridge to get to their table. It was a relaxing place to sit and talk about the day's events.

While they waited for their sushi rolls, Aly and AJ sipped green tea and looked at the flyer.

"This is not the same school as Gigi's," AJ said. "The address is different. And so is the contact information. This one says to call Melanie."

"Two girls' rock schools opening at the same time? That's some coincidence," Aly said. The waitress brought over their sushi. The girls thanked her and picked up their chopsticks.

"I wonder what Gigi will do after we leave New York," AJ said. "The police don't seem to have much hope of recovering the stolen equipment."

"Maybe there is more to this than meets the eye," Aly said, as she dipped a spicy tuna roll into a tiny bowl of soy sauce. "This might not have been a random crime. Someone might have wanted to put Gigi out of business."

"Someone like that Melanie, you mean?" AJ asked. "If that's the case, then maybe we can help find out what happened."

"Hey—we're musicians—not detectives!" Aly laughed.

"But we've got to try and help," AJ said, as she picked up another sushi piece with her chopsticks. "Gigi will have to close the school after we're gone if she doesn't get her stuff back."

Aly nodded. "I know we only just met Gigi, but I really like her. And when I think of all those little girls, ready to play guitar, getting their hearts broken . . ."

"It's tragic," AJ agreed. "That's why I think we should help, if we can."

"I'm not sure what we can do, but we can try," Aly said. "Maybe we can look around the school tomorrow—maybe the thief left some clues behind."

AJ smiled. "Now you're talking. Aly and AJ are on the case!"

"Then we'd better eat some more sushi," Aly said. "Fish is supposed to be good brain food."

AJ happily picked up some more sushi. "No problem. It's also way delicious!"

CHAPTER FOUR:
ON THE RADIO

"You've been listening to 'Insomniatic,' the title track from Aly and AJ's latest album!" The radio deejay, a guy named Manic Mike with bleached blond hair and sunglasses, shouted the words into the microphone at super speed. "If you're an Aly and AJ fan, today's your lucky day, because I've got these two lovely sisters right here in the studio this morning! Hey there, girls!"

"Hi, Mike," Aly and AJ replied.

"That's *Manic* Mike, and don't you forget it!"

the deejay replied. He pressed a button, and a loud whistle blew inside their headphones as he made his point.

Aly and AJ turned to each other and smiled. It didn't matter what city they were in—every city had a morning radio deejay with a wacky name and even wackier sound effects. It could be a little hard to take at eight o'clock in the morning.

"So, Aly and AJ, help me out. How am I supposed to tell you two ladies apart?" Manic Mike asked. "Which one of you is older?"

Aly and AJ had heard this question a million times. Many people thought they were twins because they looked so much alike. AJ liked to joke that they were the first twins born two years apart.

Aly raised her hand. "I'm Aly, and I'm older," she said. "But in a weird way, AJ's kind of like the older one. She's got the personality of a leader, and she's a lot more organized than I am."

"Aly might be messier than me, but she's really

creative," AJ added. "We might have different ways of doing things, but we always end up in the same place, if you know what I mean. We're on the same page."

"And I'm on the same page with your music. This new album is hot, hot, hot!" Manic Mike said. He pressed another button, and the girls heard the sound of sizzling bacon. "Do you have any words for your fans in the Big Apple?"

"Thanks for all your support," Aly said. "We're having a great time in New York City. So come on out to our concert Friday night at Madison Square Garden. It's going to be fun!"

"We also want to help out our friend Gigi at the Girls Rock Academy," AJ added. "If anybody has information about the theft at Gigi's school, come forward and let Gigi know."

"Fabulous, girls!" Manic Mike said. "Thanks for coming to the studio. Let's send you out with another track from *Insomniatic*!"

Mike pressed a button, and another song began to

play. Aly and AJ took off their headphones. Mike gave them a nod.

"Great job, guys. Have a terrific show on Friday," he said.

The girls thanked him and left the cramped studio. Outside the door, a guy in his early twenties paced back and forth. He wore jeans and an official Aly and AJ tour shirt. His short brown hair looked like it hadn't been brushed in a few days, but the effect was kind of cute.

"Hey, Jim!" The girls greeted their new tour manager. Fresh out of college, Jim was frantic most of the time. Managing the Insomniatic tour was his first big job.

"Aly, AJ," he said. "Nice job. I've got the tour bus downstairs. Are you sure about lending equipment to this rock school? Without the equipment, we can't have a show."

They walked down the hallway of the radio station as they talked. "It'll be fine, Jim," AJ assured him. "It's only for a few days."

"But you hardly even know this Gigi person," Jim

said, pressing the button for the elevator. "For all you know, this could be some kind of scam."

"Gigi's cool," Aly said. "Call it sisterly intuition. You really need to learn how to relax, Jim."

"Relax. Sure." But Jim's foot tapped on the elevator floor all the way to the building lobby. They walked outside, where the tour bus was parked and waiting for them. The huge bus didn't look like anything special on the outside, but inside was a Hello Kitty explosion—the beds were covered with Hello Kitty sheets and pillows; the kitchen area had Hello Kitty dishes and placemats; even the bathroom had a Hello Kitty shower curtain.

Aly and AJ flopped on the Hello Kitty couch in the middle of the bus. Jim sat across from them and flipped open a handheld wireless device.

"We need to wrap up this grand opening thing by this afternoon," Jim told them. "You have rehearsal with the band tonight. I had to reschedule a photo shoot so you could be at the rock school today."

"That's why you're the best tour manager in the world," Aly teased, and Jim blushed.

"Really? You think I'm doing a good job?" he asked.

"We wouldn't have hired you if we didn't have faith in you," AJ said. "You're doing great."

"Thanks," Jim said, blushing some more. He seemed to relax a little for the first time all morning.

A few minutes later the tour bus stopped in front of the brownstone building that housed the Girls Rock Academy. Gigi waited for them outside, and a young man stood next to her. He wore a tie-dye T-shirt; his long, brown hair was tied in a ponytail that hung down his back.

Gigi greeted the girls with a hug. "You guys are so awesome for doing this!" she gushed. She nodded to the tie-dye guy. "This is Miles. He's the other instructor here at the school."

"Hey," Miles said.

Jim climbed out of the bus, carrying a heavy

amp. "All right, where does this go?" he asked, panting heavily.

"Oh, gosh, let me help!" Gigi said. She grabbed the other end of the amp. Miles held the door open for them as they carried the amp up the stairs into the building.

"Might as well grab some guitars," AJ said. She and Aly climbed back into the bus and came back holding two guitar cases each. Miles was still holding the door open. He seemed to have decided that was his job for the morning.

Aly was chatting excitedly as they walked through the door. "I can't wait to meet the little girls who want to rock out," she told AJ. "They've got to be so cute. Oh!"

Aly bumped into someone coming through the opposite side of the door. She looked up to see a boy with sandy blond hair and the greenest eyes she'd ever seen. The boy was carrying a big instrument case. Aly recognized the shape—it was the case for a cello, a stringed instrument played with a bow.

"Sorry," Aly said.

"That's okay," the boy replied. "I can't see past this thing sometimes."

He looked down at the girls' guitar cases. "Are you students at the Girls Rock Academy?" he asked.

"Not exactly," Aly said. "We're here for the grand opening."

The boy looked surprised. "I thought that was canceled," he said. "I thought there was some stolen equipment or something."

AJ joined the conversation. "We're lending Gigi our equipment for the week. I'm AJ. My sister Aly and I are musicians. We're playing Madison Square Garden on Friday."

The boy didn't take the cue and introduce himself. An uncomfortable look crossed his face. "That's nice, I guess," he said. "I'm not really into loud music."

He squeezed past them without saying another word. Aly shot AJ a curious look.

"Very cute," she said. "But a little strange."

"Definitely," AJ said. "He acted like we were in some heavy metal band or something. I don't think I've ever heard our music described as 'loud' before."

Aly laughed. "I guess there's a first time for everything!"

CHAPTER FIVE:
AN IMPOSTOR!

They brought the guitar cases down the hall and past the classroom to a room with an open door. Gigi and Jim had placed the amp in a corner. AJ noticed that some acoustic guitars hung on hooks on the walls.

"Do those belong to the school?" she asked.

Gigi nodded. "Those were the only things that weren't stolen. Weird, right? I'm glad they didn't get stolen, but they're not enough to help me run the school."

Jim ran a hand through his hair. "There are some smaller amps in the bus. I'll go get them."

"We're right behind you," Aly said.

As they headed back to the bus, AJ noticed another brass plaque by the front door. It read Classical Music Center.

"That explains the guy with the cello," AJ remarked.

"You mean Brandon?" Gigi asked. "I see him around a lot. There's a practice space for classical musicians on the third floor. I've tried to talk to some of the kids who practice there, but they don't seem very friendly for some reason. I figured we have a lot in common, studying music and everything, but I get the feeling they don't think guitars are worth their time."

"Brandon was definitely not the friendliest guy I've met in New York," Aly agreed. "But he sure was cute."

"I guess," Gigi said. She lowered her voice a little. "If you ask me, your tour manager's the cute one."

Aly and AJ grinned at each other. It was hard to think of Jim as "cute"—he was, well, Jim. He'd become like an older brother to them.

"Don't let Jim hear you say that," AJ joked. "He'll blush, and then he'll start to stammer, and then he'll run his hand through his hair . . ."

Gigi grinned. "I'd like to see that," she said. "But I guess I should be focused on the grand opening. I was able to reach all the students to tell them that the school was opening after all. The girls should be here in about an hour."

"Then let's get this bus unloaded," AJ said.

With everyone helping they got the equipment unloaded in no time. Miles left his post at the door and began to set up the chairs in the main classroom. Jim pitched in.

"You two should relax until showtime," Gigi said. "There's not much to do now, anyway."

"Then maybe now is a good time to talk about the theft yesterday," AJ said. "Aly and I have been thinking. We'd like to help get your equipment back, if we can."

Gigi shook her head in disbelief. "You guys are way too nice. I heard you on Manic Mike's show this morning, by the way. Thanks for mentioning it. Maybe somebody will come forward."

"I hope so," AJ said. "In the meantime, we wanted to ask you about something strange we saw yesterday. This girl on the street was putting up signs for another girls' rock school."

Gigi frowned. "That's Melanie Downing," she said. "I don't know much about her, except that after I started advertising my school, she showed up here. She was really angry. She accused me of stealing her idea. That's ridiculous! I'd never even met her before. I tried to explain, but she wouldn't listen."

Aly and AJ exchanged glances. They were both thinking the same thing.

"Do you think Melanie stole the equipment so you couldn't open your school?" Aly asked.

Gigi's dark eyes widened. "I never even thought of that! I've been so worried about opening the school that I haven't been thinking clearly."

Her expression turned dark. "I feel like marching over to that school of hers right now and confronting her. I bet all my stuff is there!"

"Maybe," Aly said. "But it wouldn't be cool to accuse her without any proof. If she *is* guilty, she'd have no reason to admit it."

Gigi sighed. "You're right. But what kind of proof are we supposed to get?"

AJ took a small notebook out of her bag. "I've been working on a list of questions that might help us find out."

Aly didn't know her sister had been making a list, but she wasn't surprised. AJ loved to make lists. She said it helped her think clearly. Aly liked to imagine that her sister's brain was as well organized as her drawers, with all of her thoughts neatly folded and put away so she could easily find them.

"First of all, how did the thief get into the equipment room?" AJ asked. "Was it locked?"

"I swear I locked it the night before," Gigi said. "I'm always really careful about that."

"So then there'd have to be evidence of someone breaking the lock," Aly guessed. "Like screwdriver marks or something."

"I didn't notice anything," Gigi said. "But we can look."

They walked to the equipment room and checked the door handle. There were no marks on it at all.

"So whoever got into this door must have had a key," AJ said slowly. "Do you know if there's a security camera in the building? Or maybe a security guard?"

Gigi slapped her forehead. "We have both! There's a guard stationed in the basement most times. He watches the camera on a monitor. Why didn't I think of this before?"

She ran down the hall and entered the door to the basement. Aly and AJ followed her downstairs.

They found an elderly man sitting at a metal desk. Patches of white hair dotted his mostly bald head; he wore bottle-thick eyeglasses and a pale blue uniform.

"Hey, Mr. Willis, it's Gigi, from the guitar school," Gigi said.

The security guard smiled when he saw her. "Why, hello, Gigi. How are you?"

"Not so great," Gigi answered. "Somebody stole a bunch of stuff from my equipment room. Do you know who was on duty Sunday night?"

Mr. Willis thumbed through a notebook on his desk. "Why, it was me. I remember now. You came to see me Sunday night. You lost the key to your equipment room, remember? So I let you in."

Gigi's pale skin turned even paler. "Mr. Willis, that wasn't me. I didn't lose my key. Are you sure that's what happened?"

Mr. Willis peered at Gigi through his glasses. "Are you certain it wasn't you? It sure looked like you."

Aly gasped. "I know what happened!" she cried. "Gigi, someone impersonated you. That's how they stole your equipment!"

CHAPTER SIX:
A STICKY CLUE

Gigi looked stunned. "You mean someone dressed up like me to get into the room? That's so creepy!" She shuddered.

"Gigi, you said there was a camera in the hallway," AJ said. "Is there a security tape we could look at? Maybe we can see who it is."

Mr. Willis frowned. "There is a camera there. But you see—"

He was interrupted by Miles, who called down

from the top of the stairs. "Gigi! Are you down there? The girls are starting to arrive."

Gigi's face was troubled. She turned to the security guard. "We'll come back later. Thanks for your help."

Aly and AJ followed Gigi back to the first floor. The hallway was crowded with excited looking girls and their parents. Gigi cheered up at the sight of her students.

"Hey," she said. "Welcome to the Girls Rock Academy."

"Oh, wow! It's Aly and AJ!" someone in the crowd shouted.

The girls in the crowd began to squeal with excitement. Aly and AJ waved and smiled. Nothing made them happier than meeting their fans in person.

Gigi tried to control the excited crowd. "Please follow me into the main classroom. You'll all get to meet Aly and AJ in a few minutes."

The girls in the crowd smiled shyly and waved at Aly and AJ as they filed into the room. Aly and AJ waited in the hallway, peeking into the room to see what was in store.

Some of the girls looked as young as eight years old, and others were in their teens. A few of the girls looked like mini Gigis, with black clothes and spiky hair. But some girls wore pretty dresses; others were casual in jeans and T-shirts. A few had brought their own guitars with them. The girls might have looked different, but they all looked really excited to be there.

Gigi and Miles had set up the room just for the grand opening. Folding chairs faced the front of the room. Colorful cardboard guitars hung from the ceiling. A table in the corner held a cooler of cold sodas and water bottles, and platters of guitar-shaped cookies. A few reporters holding cameras stood against the back wall, waiting for Aly and AJ to appear.

Soon everyone was settled in. Gigi walked to the front of the room.

"Hey, everybody! It's opening day at the Girls Rock Academy. Are you ready to rock?"

The room erupted in cheers and screams.

"Fantastic," Gigi said. "In a minute, I'm going to tell you a little bit about what to expect from your classes here. But first, I have some very special guests to introduce. Let's give a big Rock Academy welcome to Aly and AJ!"

Aly and AJ walked into the room. They high-fived some of the excited girls as they made their way to the front of the room. Flashbulbs lit up the room as the photographers began to take pictures.

"Hello, Girls Rock Academy!" Aly shouted. The girls let out another cheer. "I'm Aly."

"And I'm AJ," her sister said. "We're really happy to be here today. Aly and I picked up guitars for the first time a few years ago. It was like love at first sight. We haven't put them down since."

"It's so cool that you're all learning how to play guitar," Aly added. "We need more girl rockers in the world."

"Play a song!" someone shouted.

Everyone started clapping, urging on Aly and AJ. The sisters looked at each other. They hadn't been planning to sing—but why not?

Jim must have read their minds. He ran up, holding a guitar in each hand.

"I thought you might need Artemis and Jonah," he said.

"Thanks, Jim!" the girls said. They strapped on their guitars, and gave a quick check to make sure they were in tune.

"How about 'Do You Believe in Magic'?" AJ suggested. They had covered the sixties song on their first album, *Into the Rush*, and it had been a big hit.

Aly grinned. "Let's do it!"

She strummed a chord on her guitar, and the girls launched into the song. Soon everyone in the Girls Rock Academy was rocking out.

They finished the song to applause and cheers.

"Thanks!" AJ called out. "Now let's turn things back over to Gigi. It's your turn to rip now!"

Aly and AJ grabbed a bottle of water each and hung out at the side of the room with Jim. Gigi and Miles got up and talked a little bit about the classes at the school. Then everyone began to mill around, talking excitedly and munching on guitar cookies.

"How much time do we have before rehearsal?" AJ asked Jim.

"A few hours," Jim replied. "I promised your mom you'd have time for a proper dinner beforehand. She doesn't want you girls to get run-down."

"We'll have time to eat," AJ promised. "I want to meet some of the girls here first. And we still have to finish up some business with Gigi."

"Okay," Jim said. "Just don't go far."

The sisters were drawn to a corner of the classroom where the sound of an electric guitar wailing got their attention. The sound was coming from a girl who looked to be about ten years old. Her reddish hair hung over her face as she played. She wore boots, khaki pants, and a brown T-shirt with a Fender guitar on it.

Aly and AJ watched as the girl played a series of notes up and down the guitar's long neck. She had plugged her electric guitar into a tiny amp. Her face wore a look of concentration. She didn't play every note perfectly, but she still sounded good.

"She's so cute," Aly whispered.

"She can play, too," AJ said.

A tall man with a red beard stood next to her, beaming. "That's my Shannon!"

Shannon stopped playing and looked up. She blushed a little when she saw Aly and AJ.

"Hi," she said shyly. "You guys are great. I hope I can play as good as you someday."

"Thanks," AJ replied. "You're great already. Just keep practicing."

Aly heard a small voice behind her. "I wish I could play like that."

She looked behind her to see a girl about Shannon's age with long, brown hair. She wore a pink skirt and a matching short-sleeved top.

"Hi," Aly said. "What's your name?"

"Hana," the girl replied. "It means 'flower' in Japanese."

"That's a really pretty name," Aly said. "How long have you been playing guitar?"

"I haven't started yet," Hana told her. "I've been playing piano since I was four. I like it, but I really want to play guitar. I begged my mom for lessons for the last seven years. Finally she let me."

"You know, AJ and I started out playing piano, too," Aly said. "Having a musical background really helped us learn guitar. You're starting off from a really great place."

Hana looked a little happier after hearing that. "I didn't think of that. Thanks, Aly."

Then Aly felt AJ tap her arm.

"I want to go back and see Mr. Willis," she said. "I'm dying to see that security tape."

"Good idea," Aly said. "Bye, Hana. Don't worry. I'm sure you'll be a great guitar player."

Hana smiled. "Thanks!"

Aly and AJ headed back down to the basement. Mr. Willis was filling out a crossword puzzle.

"Excuse me, Mr. Willis," AJ said. "We're Gigi's friends. Earlier we asked you about the security camera on the first floor hallway."

Mr. Willis put down his pen. "I didn't get a chance to tell you. There's something wrong with that camera. I called the maintenance company, but they haven't showed up yet."

He pointed to the monitor on the left. The screen looked blank.

AJ leaned in for a closer look. The screen was dark in the center, but she saw what looked like a video image around the edges. It was kind of weird, unless . . .

"Come on upstairs," she told Aly. "I think I know what happened."

They located the camera high on the ceiling in a corner of the hallway. AJ got a chair from the classroom and brought it under the camera. She stood on top and looked at the lens.

"Just as I thought," she said. "The lens is blocked. Somebody put chewing gum on it."

"Let me see that," Aly said. AJ climbed down, and Aly took her place. She peered down at the gum.

"It's the new Lime Invasion flavor from Bubble Blast," she said with certainty.

"How do you know that?" AJ asked. "Wait, what am I saying? Nobody knows candy better than you do."

"It's easy. It's bright green with purple flecks," Aly said, stepping down. "No other gum looks quite like that."

"Then this is a clue," AJ pointed out. "Whoever stole the equipment must chew

Lime Invasion gum. Maybe we should collect it as evidence."

"Great idea, but very gross," Aly said. "Just write it down in your notebook. We can let Mr. Willis know that the camera's not broken. And what are we supposed to do, visit every candy store in New York City and ask who's been buying Lime Invasion gum?"

"I'm not sure," AJ said. She smiled. "We're musicians, not detectives, remember?"

Set List:
- Potential
- Bullseye
- No One
- Chemicals
- ÷
- Insomniatic
- Like Woah
- Closure
- Rush

CHAPTER SEVEN:
A SKETCHY SUSPECT

Jim found the girls in the hall and reminded them it was time to go. They said good-bye to Gigi and headed back to the hotel. They ate a delicious dinner with their mom in a tiny restaurant in Little Italy, a small neighborhood in Manhattan filled with Italian restaurants. Then Jim took them to the rehearsal studio in a cab.

The studio space was in an office building around the corner from Madison Square Garden. They could hear the sound of drums and guitars before they even opened the door.

Inside, the guys in the girls' backup band were getting ready to rehearse. Tommy, a man with a braided goatee, sat behind the drums, lightly tapping the cymbals. Malcolm, the tall, thin bassist, warmed up by playing scales on his bass guitar. Brown-haired Matt tuned his electric guitar, and spiky-haired Jeffrey, who was also the musical director, was fixing a connection on his keyboard.

"Hey, guys, what's up?" AJ cried.

Aly and AJ had worked with their band since recording *Into the Rush*. They'd survived one tour together, and the girls were glad the band had signed on for the Insomniatic tour. At this point, they felt more like a family than just a band.

Jeffrey picked up a big sheet of cardboard with song titles written on it in magic marker.

"I've been working on a set list, based on our last meeting," he said. "We'll start with 'Potential Breakup Song.'"

Tommy nodded. "Good choice. I like that tune."

Aly and AJ studied the list. "I'm glad we have 'No One' on the list," Aly remarked. The song was one of their biggest hits. "It's nice to mix in some of the old stuff."

"We should practice that one," AJ suggested. "I feel like I haven't sung it in a long time."

The girls strapped on their acoustic guitars and stepped in front of the microphones. After a quick sound check, they nodded to the band. The song began with Aly and AJ strumming chords on the acoustic. Then AJ began to sing.

"I am moving through the crowd
Trying to find myself.
Feel like a guitar that's never played
Will someone strum away?"

Singing the song felt like visiting with an old friend. They finished the song, then went through the set list from beginning to end with the band. By the time rehearsal was done, the girls were feeling pretty tired.

"I'd better get you girls back to the hotel," Jim said. "Your mom—"

"—wants us to get a good night's sleep," Aly and AJ finished for him. "We know."

They said good night to the band and headed back to the hotel. They found their mom waiting in the room for them. She was hanging up a blouse in the closet.

"I was just taking a look at your wardrobe for your photo shoot tomorrow morning," Carrie told them. "Alyson, you really should learn how to hang up your clothes."

"I will, Mom," Aly said, feeling like a little girl again. She gave her mom a hug. "I'm so glad you're here on tour with us. You make every place feel just like home."

Carrie gave her a kiss on the cheek. "I wouldn't want to be anywhere else. Now you two should think about getting ready for bed. You've got a big photo shoot in the morning."

"We promise, Mom," AJ said.

The girls took their mom's advice. They quickly showered and got into some comfy pj's. Aly climbed into her bed first. She switched on the lamp next to the bed and picked up her sketchbook, which she kept on the nightstand. Aly loved to draw; she usually took her sketchbook with her everywhere, doodling people she'd met and interesting things she'd seen. The last two days had been so busy she hadn't had time to pick it up.

"What are you drawing?" AJ asked, flopping down on her own bed.

"Gigi," Aly answered. "I've been wondering how somebody might have been able to impersonate her."

Aly roughly sketched Gigi's face—her spiky hair, big, dark eyes, and friendly smile.

"Right now, Melanie seems like the most likely suspect," AJ pointed out. "She definitely has a motive for wanting to ruin Gigi's school. And to be honest, she doesn't seem very nice, does she? Gigi said she got really angry and wouldn't even listen to her explanation."

"Just what I was thinking," Aly said. She began to draw Melanie's face next, with her thin hair and quirky eyeglasses. AJ sat on the bed next to her and watched her draw.

"That looks like Melanie," AJ said.

"Now let's see what happens when I do this." Aly erased Melanie's eyeglasses. She added thick black eyeliner around the eyes, like Gigi wore. Then she erased Melanie's long hair and made it spiky on top instead.

AJ raised an eyebrow. "Wow," she said. Melanie's face was thinner than Gigi's, and her nose was longer. But if she had changed her hair and makeup, she might have been able to pass as Gigi. "Mr. Willis has awfully thick glasses. I bet Melanie could have fooled him easily."

Aly put down her pencil. "I think so, too. Maybe it's time we talk to Melanie. But how are we supposed to find her?"

"I saved the flyer, remember?" AJ answered.

"We can visit Melanie's school after our photo shoot tomorrow."

Aly grinned. "Sister, maybe you are becoming a detective after all."

CHAPTER EIGHT:
PICTURES IN THE PARK

"I can't believe this beautiful park is in the middle of such a big city," Aly remarked.

She, AJ, and their mom were walking down a path in Central Park, a large, rectangle-shaped oasis in the heart of Manhattan. It was only seven in the morning, but thanks to some Cokes, a breakfast of crunchy bacon and fresh fruit, and the crisp morning air, they felt wide-awake.

There wasn't a single cloud in the bright blue

sky overhead. The walking path was lined with trees showing off their first green leaves and showy yellow daffodils. In the distance, the tall buildings that bordered the park sparkled like silver in the sunshine.

"It's a great place for a photo shoot," AJ agreed.

"The editors at *New York Weekend* suggested it," Carrie told them. "It's so exciting that they want to do a cover shoot with you. The issue comes out on stands Friday morning, just in time for your show."

AJ studied the small map of Central Park she carried. "We're supposed to meet them at the West Drive entrance to the Sheep Meadow," she said. "I think we're getting close."

Aly pointed. "I think we're there."

Jim stood on the path up ahead, waving at them. "Hey, guys! Over here!"

They caught up to Jim. He led them off the path onto an open, green field. Although it was early in the morning, the field was dotted with people sitting on blankets. Some were reading, others were doing yoga, but most were just enjoying the early morning sunshine.

Jim led them to a small group of people from the magazine: Parvati, the art director; Alex, the photographer; and a petite girl named Kristin who was there to do their hair and makeup.

Parvati wore a black tank top tucked into her jeans. Her long, brown hair was braided down her back, and silver hoops dangled from her ears. She eyed the girls as they were introduced.

"Great outfits," she said.

Aly had on a worn-in vintage tee with a vest covered with funky buttons. A thick, tan leather belt looped around her jeans, and she wore a pair of tan boots to match. AJ had on her favorite pair of vintage jeans and the new black boots they'd found at the shoe store a few days ago. She'd layered a black tank top over a lilac one.

"Thanks," the girls replied.

"Kristin will fix you up while Alex sets up the

shot," Parvati told them. "Although you guys don't need much fixing."

Aly and AJ sat down in two tall canvas folding chairs and Kristin went to work. She added some styling lotion to Aly's wavy hair to keep it from getting frizzy, and she gave AJ's straight hair a hit of spray to keep it smooth and shiny. Both sisters tended to wear similar makeup: earth tones to bring out the gold flecks in their green eyes; a hint of blush on their cheeks; and lip gloss just a shade darker than their natural color. Kristin stepped back and looked at them when they were done.

"Perfect!" she said.

By then Parvati and Alex had set up the shot. A white blanket was spread out on the green grass.

"We want to get you on the blanket, playing your guitars," Parvati said. "We'll get a great view of New York in the background."

The girls sat down on the blanket. They had to move around a lot as Parvati tried to get them in exactly the right pose.

"Aly, try cross-legged. No, put your legs behind you. Shift a little to the left, AJ."

When she was satisfied, the girls tried to stay still as Jim handed them their guitars.

"All right, now play something," Parvati directed them. "Don't worry about looking at the camera. Just look natural."

"How can we act natural when we're twisted up like pretzels?" Aly joked. But the sisters were used to posing for the cameras by now. AJ started playing the intro to "Bullseye," and the girls soon got lost in the song while Alex snapped away.

When the song ended, they looked up and realized a small crowd had gathered around them.

"Take a break," Parvati told them. "We've got some good shots, but I'm not sure they're cover shots."

The girls spent a few minutes signing autographs for the people in the crowd. Then Parvati walked up to them.

"We'd like to get some different shots. Maybe the two of you by a tree or something," she suggested.

"Sounds good," AJ said. They moved the operation down the field to a beautiful old oak tree. Parvati had Aly and AJ stand on either side of the tree, leaning against the trunk. They tried a few different poses.

"Nice," Parvati said. "But I want a shot that shows off your personalities more, I think. I don't know if the tree is doing it for me."

"Maybe there's something else in the park we can use in the shot," AJ suggested.

Aly was scanning the field, covering her eyes with her hand to block the morning sun. She pointed into the distance. "What's that?"

"That's the Central Park carousel," Parvati explained.

"Wow, I read about that in my New York guidebook," Aly said. "The horses are all hand-painted, and they're, like, a hundred years old. They looked so beautiful in the picture."

Parvati grinned and nodded to Alex. "I think we've got our next shot."

A few minutes later they were setting up for a shoot by the carousel. It wasn't open yet, but Parvati had a quick conversation with the operator. Her kids happened to be Aly and AJ fans, so she gave them permission for a few shots.

The horses were even more spectacular up close than in the pictures Aly had seen. Each wooden horse had a colorfully painted blanket and saddle. Aly chose a brown horse with a red, blue, and green blanket. AJ sat on a white horse with a pink and purple saddle. The girls laughed as they climbed on their horses, pretending to ride them. Alex snapped picture after picture.

"Great! I think we have our cover shot!" Parvati said, clapping her hands together. "Take a break, guys."

Aly and AJ climbed off the carousel a little bit reluctantly. Their mom handed them each a bottle of water.

"That was so sweet," Carrie said. "It reminds me of when you two were little girls."

"It was really fun," Aly agreed.

Then the sound of music distracted them, as it usually did. This was live music, coming from somewhere nearby. It sounded like classical music.

"Let's check it out," AJ said.

They walked a little way down the path and saw three people sitting in folding chairs, playing their instruments. A short girl with black hair was playing the violin along with a tall, burly guy with brown hair. The girls were surprised when they recognized the boy playing cello with them—it was Brandon, the cute boy from Gigi's building.

Aly and AJ waited until the musicians finished

the tune they were playing. Aly gave a little wave. "Hi, Brandon," she said. "Guess we're bumping into each other again."

Brandon looked confused at first. Then he seemed to recognize the girls. "Oh, hi. You're, uh, Annie and Amy, right?"

"Actually, I'm Aly," she replied. "And this is my sister, AJ. Are these your friends?"

Brandon frowned a little, as though he didn't like being put on the spot. "This is Christy Sung and Victor Karlson," he said.

"Hi," Christy said in a tiny voice. Victor just grunted.

"That music you guys were playing was amazing," AJ said, trying to break the ice. "Aly and I play piano, you know. We love all kinds of music."

"Thanks," Brandon said blandly.

Aly and AJ exchanged glances. They were just trying to be friendly, but Brandon and his friends seemed a little standoffish. Or maybe they were just shy?

Aly made one last attempt at friendship. "AJ and I are just finishing up a photo shoot," she said. "Do you guys want to go grab a coffee or something? We'd love to hear more about the music you played."

Brandon's face colored. "No, thanks," he said quickly. "We've got a lot of, uh, stuff to do."

"Okay, then," Aly said. "See you around, maybe."

CHAPTER NINE:
FRIEND OR FOE?

"Okay. That was weird," AJ said, as they walked back to the carousel.

"We've had people act nervous around us before," Aly reminded her.

"Yeah, but usually those are fans of ours. And the kids from the Classical Music Center are definitely not fans!" AJ said.

Carrie and Jim walked over to them. "You did a fantastic job this morning," Carrie said, putting her arms around them both. "The magazine cover is going to look great!"

"For sure!" Jim added. "What do you have planned for the rest of the day? Believe it or not, you've got some free time in your schedule."

"We were hoping to go back to the Girls Rock Academy," AJ said. "We wanted to look around some more and see if we could give Gigi a hand."

Carrie nodded. "If that's what you want to do, go enjoy yourselves."

"But don't forget about rehearsal tonight," Jim reminded them.

"Don't worry, Jim," Aly said. "We'll be there!"

After kissing Carrie good-bye and assuring Jim again that they'd be on time for practice that night, Aly and AJ left Central Park.

"Before we go back to the Academy, I think it's time we pay a visit to our number-one suspect," AJ said.

"We should definitely check out Melanie's school

and ask her a few questions," Aly said. "But judging by the way she treated us on the street the other night, I don't think she'll be thrilled to see us!"

AJ shrugged. "We've got to check it out. It's almost eleven now. We'll stop by quickly before lunch." She pulled the flyer from her jeans pocket. "I've got the address right here, so let's go."

The girls caught a cab and reached Melanie's school in twenty minutes. It was a quiet ride, nothing like the ride they'd had with Murray.

The taxi dropped them off in front of a brownstone building, just a few blocks away from Gigi's school.

The girls climbed the stairs and stood in front of the door. It was locked, so they'd have to be buzzed in. AJ scanned the list of businesses and people who lived in the building.

"Here it is, the School for Girls Who Rock," AJ said. She pushed the bell next to the school's name.

"Yes?" Melanie's voice came over the intercom.

"Melanie? It's Aly and AJ. We'd really like to talk

to you," Aly said in her friendliest voice possible.

There was silence for a moment. Then the buzzer sounded.

The girls opened the door and walked into the hallway. The brownstone was a five-story walk-up, and it didn't look like there was an elevator. Luckily, Melanie's school was located on the second floor.

The girls climbed the stairs. There weren't many windows, and the hallways seemed kind of dark and depressing. The door to the school was the first one on the right. AJ knocked.

The door slowly swung open. Melanie stood there, wearing the same cat's-eye glasses, torn jeans, and boots that the girls had seen her in the first time they had met. But now she had on a vintage-looking jersey with a picture of the 1950s actor James Dean on it. Underneath his image it said REBEL. There was a look of surprise on her face.

"What do you guys want?" she asked.

"Do you think we could come in just for a second

and talk to you?" AJ asked, hoping she sounded casual.

Melanie nodded and opened the door wider. AJ and Aly scooted past her and into a large room. It was the exact opposite of the dark hallway and staircase. The room had high ceilings and large windows that let in a lot of light. It was painted a bright purple. Colored squares of yellow, light blue, and hot pink were painted around the room. Black-and-white sketches of guitars, keyboards, musical notes, and boom boxes filled the squares. Tables, chairs, and musical stands were scattered around the room. Electric and acoustic guitars and amps were lined up against the far wall.

"This is awesome!" Aly said as she looked around the room. "Who painted this?"

"I did," Melanie said. She shut the door behind them. "Have a seat."

"So that means you're a musician and an artist," AJ commented as the girls sat down on two of the metal folding chairs. "Just like Aly."

"You like to draw?" Melanie asked. Her voice sounded a little less hostile.

"Since I was a kid," Aly said. "I keep a sketchbook with me wherever I go." She almost started to take the sketchbook from her bag, then remembered the last thing she sketched in it—Melanie's face. She stopped herself just in time. "This room is amazing," she said instead.

"Thanks," Melanie said. But her face still wore a frown. "Why are you here?"

"We're musicians, too, remember? We were curious about your school," AJ said. "How long have you been open?"

"I'm not officially open yet," Melanie said. "I can't be. I don't have any students. Gigi stole them all."

"That doesn't sound like Gigi," Aly said. "Are you sure that's what happened?"

Melanie sighed. "Opening this school has been my dream. I've been planning it for years, but didn't have the money and couldn't find the right space. Finally, when everything started to come together for me, I found out about the Girls Rock Academy. I was just moving into this place, getting it painted and ready. I couldn't believe it! Gigi was already advertising and signing up students. Now all the students who would have signed up for my school went to Gigi's. Just because she opened first."

AJ leaned forward. "I know you don't know us," she said, "but you have to trust us on this. Gigi is a really nice person. She had no idea you were opening a rock school."

"She had no way of knowing," Aly added. "She was doing the same thing you were—concentrating on getting her school open and making it the best."

"I guess she told you how I went over to see her," Melanie said. Aly and AJ nodded. "I didn't mean to yell and get so upset. But it's hard to sit back and watch my dream die." Her eyes filled with tears as she spoke those last words.

AJ understood where Melanie was coming from;

her desire to see her dream come true had made her act out of character. AJ had a hunch there was a really nice person under that scowling exterior. "Don't give up," she urged. "Have you gotten any response from the flyers you posted?"

Melanie shook her head. "Not one phone call."

"You've got to have faith," Aly said. "Just look at this room! It's so inspiring. It makes me want to jam."

"Why don't we?" Melanie asked. The girls saw her smile for the first time. "I have to admit that I love your music. When I heard that Gigi got you two to come to her grand opening, it made me even madder! That's why I was so rude to you when we met on the street the other day. I'm sorry."

"It's okay," AJ said. "We understand."

Aly got up and walked toward the guitars. "Now what should we play?"

"How about some classic rock?" Melanie asked. She picked up a black-and-white guitar and plugged it into an amp. "You know who you two have always reminded me of a little? Heart."

Aly and AJ smiled at the compliment. The sisters had always admired Heart, a band fronted by two sisters, Ann and Nancy Wilson. They were really big in the 1980s, known for their rocking sound and power ballads.

"Then let's try a little 'Barracuda,'" AJ said.

Melanie began to play while Aly accompanied her. AJ sang lead vocals and Aly joined in to back her up. The song was a high-powered, guitar shredding, thundering masterpiece.

"Oh, Barracuda!" AJ sang the last note.

"Yeah!" Melanie whooped. For the first time since meeting her, she seemed truly happy. "That was incredible!"

"*You* were incredible," Aly said with awe in her voice. "You rocked that song. You are an excellent guitar player."

Melanie turned red. "Thanks," she said.

"That was wild!" AJ said. "But maybe we could do something slower now."

Melanie picked up an acoustic guitar. "Help yourselves!" The three girls sat on the floor and had a mellow, free-flowing jam session, talking and laughing throughout.

Suddenly, AJ glanced at her watch.

"It's almost one o'clock!" she said. "We really should go and have some lunch."

They put the guitars back and walked to the door.

"Thanks for stopping by," Melanie said. "Again, I'm sorry for being rude."

"It's okay," AJ said. "We really do hope your school is a huge success. You are super talented. Any girls who want to rock could learn a lot from you!"

Again, they got to see Melanie smile. It brightened her whole face. "Thanks. Come back anytime!"

After saying their good-byes, the girls started to walk out the door. Then Aly remembered something she had wanted to do. She reached into her pocket and turned around.

"Hey, do you want some Lime Invasion gum?" she asked, holding out the package.

Melanie shook her head. "Thanks, but I don't chew gum."

The girls left the building. Once they were down the stairs and on the street, they stopped to talk.

"That was smart to ask her if she wanted some Lime Invasion," AJ said. "We had so much fun after a while that I forgot we were there because she was a suspect!"

"I know. I almost did, too," Aly said. "And I can't help but wonder if we were on the wrong track with Melanie."

"Melanie seems pretty smart. She might have known why I was asking her about the gum, and lied about it," AJ mused. "But if she was telling the truth, then she wasn't the person who blocked the security camera. And if Melanie didn't do it, then who did?"

CHAPTER TEN:
A NEW SUSPECT?

"Mmmmm, New York pizza," Aly said, holding up a slice of hot pizza to her mouth.

"There's nothing like it!" AJ agreed as she grabbed a slice of her own and folded it before she took a bite.

They were sitting in a small pizza place just a few doors down from Melanie's school. Tucked into a cozy booth with a cheery red and white striped tablecloth, the girls were discussing their visit with Melanie.

"Thanks to your drawings, we know Melanie

could impersonate Gigi," AJ said between bites.

"And what better motive could someone have than wanting to make their dream come true?" Aly asked. "If Gigi goes out of business, all those girls will have no place to go to school. Melanie could sign them all up and make her school a success."

"But after getting to know her," AJ said, "I can't imagine her doing something like that."

"Who knew that under all that rudeness she was such a cool girl and gnarly guitar player?" Aly asked. "I'm not so sure she did it, either."

"But then who?" AJ asked. She reached into her purse and pulled out her notes about the theft.

"The facts," she announced as she read from her notebook. "Gigi first noticed all of her equipment was stolen Monday morning, the day of the grand opening."

"Hmmm," AJ continued. She paused thoughtfully and screwed up her face. "That's wrong."

"What do you mean?" Aly asked.

"Not all of the school's equipment was stolen," she said as her eyes scanned her notes. "The acoustic guitars were left behind."

"Why wouldn't a thief take them, too?" Aly wondered. "They are worth at least a couple of hundred dollars each."

"Which is why I don't think this is a random crime," AJ said. "A common thief would either break the lock or wait for an opportunity like someone leaving the door open. Who would go to all the trouble to impersonate Gigi?"

"And if it was some thief just looking to make a few bucks, why not take the acoustic guitars?" Aly asked.

AJ sighed and shook her head. "Melanie still seems like the only suspect. But since I can't believe she did it, there is only one thing left to do."

Aly nodded. "Go back to the Girls Rock Academy and do some more investigating!" Then she bit into her pizza.

The girls left the pizza place and walked the few blocks to the school. Since it was such a beautiful day, the windows were open and they could hear the sounds of guitars drifting through the air.

They walked into the building and peered into the first classroom. Gigi sat in the middle of the room, holding a guitar. She was demonstrating finger placement. Mostly younger girls and a few teenagers sat around, holding guitars of their own and copying Gigi's movements.

"And that is a G chord!" Gigi announced with a smile. "Or the Gigi chord, as I like to call it!" The girls laughed and tried the chord for themselves.

Gigi glanced up and saw Aly and AJ standing in the doorway. She walked over while her students practiced.

"Aly, AJ, hi!" she exclaimed. "You are just in time to see the Girls Rock Academy in action. I'm teaching a beginners' class right now, and Miles is down the hall teaching the advanced class. Do you want to sit in?"

"We should split up. Maybe we'll learn something," AJ whispered to Aly. She turned to Gigi. "I'd like to see what the advanced class is doing," she said.

"Sure. I'd like to stick around here," Aly said.

AJ headed down the hallway to Miles's classroom. Aly took a seat in the back of the room while Gigi resumed teaching.

"Okay, guys," Gigi said to her class. "Keep practicing what we learned today. I'm going to walk around and check everyone's finger placement. Aly, you want to help?"

"I'd love to." Aly smiled. The girls were so cute!

Aly looked around the room. She spotted Hana, the little girl she had spoken to at the grand opening. Hana was sitting in the corner. She had put her guitar on the stand and was sitting hunched over with her elbows on her knees and her chin in her hands, looking sad.

"What's the matter, Hana?" Aly knelt down next to her.

"I'm just not getting it," Hana said quietly. Today

she wore a denim skirt and a Hello Kitty T-shirt with pink Crocs on her feet. She didn't even look up at Aly.

"First of all, I love your shirt," Aly said. "Second of all, don't be so blue. Mastering any kind of musical instrument takes a lot of time and patience. You should know that from playing the piano."

Hana looked up at Aly. "The piano was a lot easier for me. The guitar is so different!"

"Just think of a guitar as a piano flipped on its side," Aly suggested. "Here, let me show you." She guided Hana's hands and fingers up and down the guitar neck.

While Aly was helping Hana, AJ was watching the more experienced guitar players in Miles's class. After showing them the chord changes from the song "Since U Been Gone" by Kelly Clarkson, he slouched into a chair.

"Now you can all just chill and practice," he said before slipping his iPod out of his pocket and putting the earphones in his ears. He closed his eyes and started bobbing his head to the beat of whatever music he was listening to.

AJ wasn't very impressed. *What kind of teacher does that?* she thought to herself. She glanced around the room as the sounds of "Since U Been Gone" began to fill the air. She spotted Shannon, the girl they'd met the other day, wearing a deep frown as she concentrated on the sheet music on the stand in front of her. Her guitar sat comfortably in her lap. She was wearing an old AC/DC concert T-shirt and a pair of camouflage capri pants with black Converse sneakers.

"Shannon, how's it going?" Aly asked.

"Ugh!" Shannon muttered. "I can play this song if I do it by listening to it. But when I try to read the music, I get all confused and nothing makes sense!"

"You don't know how to read music yet?" AJ asked.

Shannon shook her head.

"Don't worry, you'll learn," AJ said. "You've just got to keep trying."

"I know, but I want to jam!" Shannon moaned. "Just like AC/DC. My dad gave me this shirt. He's been playing their CDs for me since I was a tiny baby. That's why I started playing guitar. Angus Young is the best guitar player in the universe."

AJ smiled. AC/DC was a heavy metal band that became famous in the 1970s. If the people from the Classical Music Center heard Shannon rocking AC/DC down here, they would not be happy. Now *that* was loud music!

"Don't get discouraged," AJ told her. "It's only the first day of class. Give yourself some time to learn."

She sat down next to Shannon and helped go over the sheet music with her. Before long, parents began to arrive to pick up their children. Shannon said good-bye to AJ as she packed up her stuff and left with her dad.

Miles opened his eyes and looked around. He pulled the iPod headphones out of his ears.

"Great. Now I can go home," he said to AJ. He began gathering the sheet music and putting it away.

"How do you like teaching here?" AJ asked. She couldn't help being curious about him. Why would somebody who didn't seem to like teaching want to teach guitar to kids?

"Whatever. It's just a way to earn some money," he said with a shrug. "I'm more interested in making my own music than teaching. I'll probably be as famous as you and your sister someday. All I need is some money."

"For what?" AJ asked.

"So I can record a CD. As soon as I get the money saved up, it's bye-bye, Girls Rock Academy," he answered. He put the last music stand away and nodded toward AJ. "I'm out of here. Later." Then he walked out the door.

AJ followed. She saw Aly coming out of Gigi's classroom and grabbed her, pulling her into the equipment room. It was empty, so they could talk in private.

"That was so much fun," Aly said. "The girls are adorable, and they're trying so hard to learn."

"They are," AJ said. "But I think I found someone even more interesting."

"Who?" Aly asked.

"Miles," AJ told her.

"Uh-oh," Aly said. "Don't tell me you've got a crush on him!"

"No!" AJ gave Aly a playful swat on the shoulder. "What I mean is, Miles didn't seem very interested in teaching the class. Afterward I was talking to him. He doesn't like it here very much. In fact, as soon as he earns enough money to record a CD, he said he's quitting."

"Hmmm." Aly looked thoughtful. "Do you think he wants the money so badly he'd steal Gigi's equipment for it?"

"It's a possibility," AJ said. "It looks like we have another suspect!"

CHAPTER ELEVEN:
THE RED GUITAR

Aly and AJ took a few steps out of the equipment room before they stopped short. Gigi was standing in the hallway with Brandon in front of her. She looked upset.

"I'll expect an improvement tomorrow," Brandon said. He turned and walked off, looking angry.

Aly and AJ approached Gigi.

"What was that about?" Aly asked.

Gigi let out a huge sigh and ran her fingers

95

through her spiky black hair. "If I didn't know better, I'd think the Girls Rock Academy is jinxed! Between losing my equipment and now having to deal with the people from the Classical Music Center, I don't know how I'm going to make this school a success! Brandon was complaining about the noise."

"The noise?" AJ asked. "We could hear the guitars a little bit with the windows open but it certainly wasn't too loud."

"Try telling that to Brandon," Gigi said. "He said it interfered with their practice upstairs. If I don't do something about it, he said he'd complain to the landlord."

"He did say he didn't like loud music," Aly remembered. "The day we were moving the equipment into the building."

"I'm not going to let it bother me," Gigi said. "Today was a great day and my class was fantastic. The girls were so excited to learn. I should ask Miles how his class went. Have you seen him?"

"He left already," AJ said. "Something about having to get home."

"I'll check in with him tomorrow," Gigi said. "And I guess I'll have to shut the windows then, too. Maybe that will make Brandon happy. How's the investigation going?"

Aly and AJ filled her in on the Lime Invasion bubble gum clue and their meeting with Melanie. Both of them agreed, without having to say anything to each other, not to mention their suspicions about Miles. Gigi had enough to worry about!

After getting hugs and thanks from Gigi, Aly and AJ headed out of the school and back to their hotel for a pit stop before rehearsal. They decided to walk.

The streets were getting crowded with men and women dressed in business suits hurrying home. Others were pushing baby carriages and quite a few people were walking dogs. AJ and Aly had fun people-watching as they strolled through the city.

After seeing countless adorable babies and too-cute pups, a woman walking a pug caught their eye. The woman looked ordinary enough in a pale blue knit dress. But the pug was hysterical! It had on a frilly pink tutu with a matching bow on its head and a pink rhinestone-studded collar.

Aly and AJ laughed.

"Your dog is so cute," Aly said.

The woman looked up. She let out a shriek.

"Oh my gosh! You're Aly," she said. "And you're AJ! We love your music. Isn't that right, Mrs. Puggy?" She bent down and scooped up the dog and cuddled it to her cheek.

"Mrs. Puggy just loves Aly and AJ," she said while talking in a high baby voice. "Isn't that right, Mrs. Puggy?" The dog glared at Aly and AJ. It did not look amused.

"Thanks," Aly said. She put out her hand to Mrs. Puggy. The dog growled and showed her teeth.

"Yikes!" Aly exclaimed. She pulled her hand away.

"Oh, I'm so sorry," the woman said, talking normally. Then she started in with the baby talk again. "Mrs. Puggy, that wasn't very nice!"

"Maybe Mrs. Puggy isn't in the mood to meet us right now," AJ said politely. "But it was nice meeting you."

The girls walked away. They waited until the woman and Mrs. Puggy were out of sight before they doubled over laughing.

"I guess Mrs. Puggy won't be joining our fan club anytime soon," AJ said between snorts. "I wish we had a video camera. Mom's never going to believe this one!"

They continued on their way, and after walking for about five blocks they passed a small guitar shop. The front window was crowded with acoustic and electric guitars. The sign over the door said IZZY'S GUITARS. JAMMIN' SINCE 1968.

"Wow!" Aly said. "Would you look at that? They've got a lot of vintage guitars."

"Luckily we've got a few minutes," AJ said. "Let's go inside."

When they opened the door a bell chimed. The store was small, but every inch was packed with equipment. Guitars hung from the ceiling and the walls. They were also on stands on the floor, fighting for space with stacks of amps and other equipment.

"Look!" AJ cried, pointing at the ceiling. "A 1957 Fender Stratocaster electric guitar!" The valuable guitar hung from the ceiling, too high to touch. The body was made of two-toned wood that was black around the edges and faded to a natural tone in the center. It had a neck made of smooth maple.

"They've also got a 1954 Gibson Les Paul," Aly said. The black guitar with cream trim was also hung out of reach.

But AJ had her sights on an acoustic guitar hanging from the wall.

"It's a beauty," AJ breathed. "The Martin Eric Clapton Signature Acoustic guitar!"

Aly stood with her sister to admire the guitar. It was made out of rosewood, and the ebony fingerboard had a diamond-and-square pattern in abalone pearl. She looked at the price tag.

"Four thousand dollars! I bet it's still way cheaper than the Strat or the Gibson," she said.

Melanie

"That's okay. Artemis and Jonah are the best guitars, anyway," AJ said. "But I wouldn't mind trying this one out." She looked around for a clerk to help. Even though the store was tiny, it was difficult to see with all the merchandise packing every available surface.

She began to make her way toward the back of the store with Aly following, but a familiar voice stopped them both in their tracks.

"It's Melanie!" AJ whispered to Aly.

They peeked over a

stack of amps and saw Melanie talking to a man standing behind a glass display counter. He had a long, scraggly gray beard and long grayish-brown hair pulled back into a ponytail. He wore a flannel shirt and jeans.

"What do you think you could give me for it, Izzy?" Melanie asked.

"Let me see," Izzy said. He opened the case and pulled out a red electric guitar. He eyed the instrument. "It's a Gibson SG special, pretty new. They retail brand-new for about seven hundred bucks, so I can't give you that much for it. It's a pretty common guitar and I've already got a few. The best I can offer is two hundred."

As Melanie and Izzy negotiated a price, Aly whipped out her sketchbook and quickly made a sketch of the guitar. Izzy opened the cash register and gave Melanie a stack of bills. She pocketed the money and turned to leave. Aly and AJ ducked behind the amps so she wouldn't see them.

The bell on the door chimed as Melanie left. Aly and AJ stood up and exchanged looks. They were both thinking the same thing. Melanie was selling a guitar. Could it be one of the stolen guitars?

"I really like Melanie," AJ said. "But it looks like she's a suspect again!"

"We need to show this sketch to Gigi," Aly said. "Maybe she can identify it as one of her missing guitars. Do you think we should go back and see if she's still at the school?"

AJ shook her head. "While we're trying to be detectives, we've still got a show at Madison Square Garden to worry about," Aly replied. "We'd better get a move on. Jim will freak if we're late for practice!"

CHAPTER TWELVE:
A DREAM COME TRUE

The girls decided to catch a cab to their hotel so they could freshen up before practice. After all, it had been a really long day!

They each took a quick shower and got dressed. Since they wanted to be comfortable, they put on their oldest, most comfy jeans. AJ paired hers with a racerback tank. It was black and had a picture of an electric guitar on the back. Since it was getting cooler out, she pulled on a gray hoodie with the Rolling Stones' logo on the back.

Aly grabbed a supersoft baby doll tank with lace trim. It was worn-in and had a few carefully placed distressed holes. She grabbed a hoodie, too—a black one with cartoon pictures of smiling pieces of sushi all over it.

"I feel so much better," AJ said. "Are you ready?"

"Let's go!" Aly replied. They left the hotel and took a cab to the studio.

"So," AJ said to her sister as the cab sped through the city streets. "Do you think Melanie is the thief after all?"

"I don't know," Aly said. "But it doesn't look good. Why was she selling that guitar? As soon as we get a chance, we'll have to show the picture to Gigi. If it is one of the missing guitars, Melanie will have some explaining to do."

The cab dropped them off in front of the office building where the studio was. They entered the studio to find everyone there and ready.

Jim smiled in relief. "You are right on time! Not that I was worried or anything, but, you know . . ."

"Oh, Jim!" Aly said. "When will you learn to relax? Hey, guys!" she said to the band.

The band greeted them with cheery hellos. Everyone was psyched about the big gig at Madison Square Garden. Now it was only days away!

Jack hit a note on his keyboard and held it. "That's an E," he said to Malcolm and Matt. Malcolm was holding his bass and Matt had his guitar. They were tuning their instruments to the note Jeffrey had just played.

Malcolm nodded. "Sounds good."

Meanwhile, Tommy was tightening and loosening the skins on his drums, making sure they were perfectly in tune.

The girls strapped on their acoustic guitars and asked Jeffrey to play the E note again. They wanted to make sure they were perfectly in sync with the rest of the band.

"Let's get warmed up," Tommy suggested. He began to beat out a funky groove. Malcolm joined in on the bass.

Matt, Aly, and AJ came in on guitar, and soon Jeffrey was playing along. They jammed out a fresh, groovy sound.

The music ended. Jim clapped.

"That was a great," he said. "And it wasn't even a real song!"

AJ looked thoughtful. "I did like that," she said. She grabbed her notebook and made a few notes. "I'll have to remember some of those sounds when we're writing our next album."

"Should we run through the set list?" Matt asked.

"Let's do it!" Aly replied.

As the music played, the world seemed to disappear. Lost in the notes and lyrics, there were only the sounds of their voices and the guitars, bass, drums, and keyboards. Thoughts of stolen equipment, suspects, and Mrs. Puggy were far, far away.

Halfway through the set they launched into "Rush," a song from their album *Into the Rush.*

"Don't let nobody tell you, your life is over, Be every color that you are, Into the rush now, You don't

have to know how, Know it all before you try," AJ and Aly sang together.

Time flew by, and before they knew it they had gone through the entire set.

"That felt good!" AJ said.

"I feel like I'm coming out of some kind of trance," Aly said. "I totally lost myself in the music."

"That's what made it so great," Jeffrey said. "No one was thinking too hard. We just let the music do the talking."

"You were all fantastic," Jim said. "The show is going to be great!"

"But we do have a few other things we should talk about," Jeffrey added. "Like, did you have anything you were planning to say to the audience in between songs?"

Aly and AJ shrugged. "I hadn't really thought about it," Aly said.

"Usually I like to have a plan, but we probably want to keep it fresh," AJ answered. "I don't want us to sound scripted or anything."

"That's a good point," Jeffrey said. "But you might want to look over your set list and see if there is anything special you might want to mention about certain songs. You know, your inspirations, any funny stories about the writing or the recording of it, that kind of thing."

"I always like when we do that," Aly said. "Each song means a lot to us."

AJ nodded in agreement. "We'll talk it over together."

"Okay," Jim said, walking over to Aly and AJ. "Then I guess we're done here for the night."

"Ah, sleep!" Aly said. "I can't wait for my head to hit the pillow."

AJ held back a yawn. "Me too. It's been a busy day!"

"I hope you've got energy for one last surprise," Jim said.

Aly's eyes grew wide. "I love surprises! What is it?"

"Come with me and I'll show you," he told them.

The girls were both now wide-awake. What could Jim have planned?

"I was hoping we could walk, but since you are both so tired, we'll grab a cab," Jim said as they walked outside. He hailed a cab and got in for a short ride. The cab let them out only a few blocks away— right in front of Madison Square Garden!

He walked into a side entrance. The girls followed. After talking to a security guard, they were ushered backstage. It was quiet. There was no show tonight and the place was empty.

"Ladies." He bowed and gestured to the stage doors. "It's all yours."

AJ and Aly slowly walked out onto the stage. Thousands and thousands of empty seats surrounded them. The indoor arena was shaped like an oval, with seating on every side of the stage.

"Wow," Aly whispered. "Imagine all of those seats filled with people."

"I feel so small standing here," AJ answered in hushed tones. "I can't believe we are going to be playing the Garden."

"What are we whispering for?" Aly asked. "This is a dream come true! Let's shout!"

AJ let out a cheer. Aly pretended to hold a microphone. "Hello, New York!" she yelled. Her voice echoed in the vacant stadium.

The girls laughed and gave each other a big hug.

"This is the best," AJ said. "And I'm so glad I'm sharing every minute of it with my sister."

"Me too," Aly said. "Who else would I want to rock New York with?"

CHAPTER THIRTEEN:
A MISSING SUSPECT

"They don't make bagels like this in California," Aly remarked. She and AJ were sitting in a crowded bagel shop near their hotel. People rushed in and out, grabbing bagels and coffee on the way to work. The sisters were getting a quick breakfast themselves. Jim had scheduled a whirlwind of publicity interviews that afternoon for them, but they hoped to spend some time discussing their latest clues.

Between bites of cinnamon raisin bagel with

walnut cream cheese, Aly sketched Miles in her book. She drew his face first, then added Gigi's spiky hair and eye makeup. She passed the sketchbook to AJ across the table.

AJ put down her whole wheat bagel with veggie cream cheese and looked at the drawing.

"I guess Miles kind of looks like Gigi, if he went to all that trouble to change his appearance," AJ said. "But Miles is really tall and skinny. I know Mr. Willis can't see very well, but would he make such a big mistake?"

Aly sighed. "Probably not. But I hate to think that Melanie is guilty. I'm really starting to like her."

"Me too," AJ said. "But it's a little weird that we saw her selling that guitar. I'm anxious to show your sketch to Gigi. Then we'll know for sure."

"Just a few bites left," Aly said. They finished breakfast, left the shop, and headed for Gigi's school. AJ called Jim from her cell phone.

"Your mom and I will pick you up at eleven thirty," he told them. "We've got a busy afternoon."

"We'll be ready," AJ assured him. "This won't take long."

It was another bright, cool spring morning. The walk to the school didn't take long. When they got there, Gigi opened the door for them. She looked upset, just like she had the day they first met her.

"What's wrong?" Aly asked. A horrible thought came over her. "Did our equipment get stolen?"

Gigi shook her head. "No, it's not that bad. It's Miles. He just called and said he was quitting! No explanation at all. Class starts in fifteen minutes. I don't know what I'm going to do."

"That's terrible," AJ said. She glanced at Aly. This was definitely suspicious behavior on Miles's part. Did he quit because he had enough money to record his CD—money he got from stealing Gigi's equipment?

"Gigi, don't worry. We'll teach Miles's class for you. At least for today," Aly offered.

AJ was surprised at her sister's offer. "But Aly, we've got interviews all day."

"We have time to teach one lesson," Aly pointed out. "Come on, it'll be fun!"

"You're right," AJ agreed. She took her notebook from her bag. "Miles was using sheet music with the class. I have the music for 'Bullseye' here in my notebook. That's got some sweet guitar parts. Gigi, can you make copies?"

Gigi nodded. "The office on the third floor lets me borrow theirs."

Gigi took the page from AJ's notebook and headed up to make copies. The girls talked about how they could teach the class. Gigi quickly returned.

"Here you go," she said, handing the copies to them. "This is totally awesome of you, once again. What would I do without you?"

AJ grinned. "It's for a good cause," she said. "Besides, Aly's right. It's going to be fun."

"Oh, hey, I almost forgot," Aly said quickly, digging into her bag. "The whole reason we came here in the first place. We saw something pretty suspicious yesterday."

She showed Gigi the sketch of the red guitar. "Does this look familiar?"

"That's a Gibson SG special. One of my favorites—until it got stolen," Gigi replied. Then her eyes widened. "Why? Did you see it somewhere?"

"We were in Izzy's guitar shop the other day," AJ told her. "Melanie was there, selling it."

"I knew it!" Gigi cried. "She stole my stuff, and now she's selling it! That's all the proof we need!"

"It does look bad for Melanie," AJ admitted. "But Izzy did say it's a pretty common guitar. Maybe—"

"She's guilty. I've known it all along," Gigi fumed. "Thanks for helping me figure this out. I'm going to go over there right after class. She won't get away with this."

Aly frowned. "Gigi, I don't know if that's such a good idea."

"You might want to calm down a little bit first," Aly suggested.

But the girls didn't have time to talk Gigi out of it.

The guitar students started pouring through the front door, and the scene became chaotic when the advanced students learned Aly and AJ would be teaching them that morning. Aly and AJ headed into the classroom to set up for the class.

Aly grabbed one of the acoustic guitars and began to tune it. They'd decided that Aly would demonstrate the chords on the guitar while AJ talked about the song and explained how to play it. The students came in, talking in excited whispers. They set up their guitars and music stands.

AJ walked around, passing out the copies of the music. She grinned at Shannon, who was plugging her electric guitar into a tiny amp. The young girl was wearing a black T-shirt with silver skulls on it today. She smiled shyly at AJ.

When AJ finished, she stood in front of the group. "Hey, everybody. Aly and I are excited to be teaching you today. We thought we'd show you how to play one of our favorite new songs, 'Bullseye.'"

"That song rocks!" one of the girls called out.

AJ laughed. "Thanks. Now we're going to show you how to rock it."

Aly played the opening notes of the song, and AJ talked the girls through playing them. It sounded really cool to hear a whole room of musicians playing their song.

AJ noticed that Shannon did really well when Aly played the notes first. But when AJ asked the girls to play the next measure on their own, Shannon looked confused. She played some notes, but they were in the wrong key.

AJ walked up to her. "Shannon, is everything okay?"

Shannon sighed. "It's like I told you yesterday. I've never had to read music before," she explained. "I've always done it by ear. I tried to learn the notes yesterday after class, but I'm still pretty confused."

"You'll get the hang of it soon," AJ promised. While the rest of the class was playing, she spent a few minutes with Shannon, showing her the notes of the major chords. Shannon relaxed a little after that.

Before they knew it, Gigi entered the room and announced that class was over. The students all groaned with disappointment.

"Thanks, everybody. We had a great time!" AJ called out.

Gigi approached them. "Thanks again. I owe you guys big-time."

"It was really amazing," Aly said. "It reminded me so much of when we were learning how to play. It seemed like we'd never be good at it."

AJ nodded toward Shannon. "I hope they don't get discouraged. Shannon could be a great guitar player. She's just not good at reading music."

"That's like Hana, in Gigi's class," Aly said. "Only she's got the opposite problem. She plays piano, and she's really good at reading music, but she has trouble handling the guitar. I don't want her to get discouraged, either."

Aly looked at her sister. "You know, the main thing that kept me going was you, AJ. We always helped each other. It's a shame those girls don't have a sister to help them out."

As soon as the words came out, Aly's eyes got wide. AJ got an excited look in her eyes, too.

"Are you thinking what I'm thinking?" Aly asked.

"Always." AJ nodded.

They ran up to Shannon. "Come on," AJ told her. "There's someone we'd like you to meet."

CHAPTER FOURTEEN:
A SUSPICIOUS SNACK

AJ grabbed Shannon's hand and led her down the hall to Gigi's classroom. Aly ran ahead and tapped Hana on the shoulder.

Both girls looked confused as Aly and AJ introduced them to each other.

"Hana, this is Shannon. Shannon, this is Hana."

"Hi," Hana said. She wrapped a long strand of her black hair around her finger.

"Hey," Shannon said shyly. Then both girls looked

up expectantly at Aly and AJ.

Aly knelt down to get on their level. "AJ and I thought you guys should meet each other," she said. "We were talking about how lucky we were to have each other when we were learning how to play guitar. We both helped each other."

"That's nice," Hana said. "I wish I had a sister."

"Me too," Shannon added. "I'm stuck with three brothers."

"That's why we wanted to introduce you," AJ said. "Shannon, you need help reading music. And Hana's really good at that. But Hana needs help handling the guitar. That's something *you're* really good at."

Shannon nodded.

"Maybe you could practice together," Aly suggested.

"I could really use help," Hana admitted. "My mom brings me here from New Jersey, though. I bet you live in New York."

"No way!" Shannon said. "I live in New Jersey, too."

The girls started to talk excitedly and realized they lived close to each other. Aly and AJ stepped back.

"I think this is going to work out," AJ said.

"Who knows?" Aly mused. "Maybe they'll form their own group when they get older. We could let them tour with us! That would be so cool."

Gigi was rushing around the classroom, hurriedly gathering up the equipment and putting things away. She had a dark look on her face, and Aly and AJ knew where she was headed.

AJ looked at her watch. "Jim and Mom will be here any minute. I wish we could go over to Melanie's with Gigi, though. I'm worried about what might happen."

"I still don't want to believe Melanie did it," Aly said. "It's really weird that Miles quit. I wish we had some way to track him down."

"I guess there's not much more we can do," AJ said. "We'd better head outside."

They waved good-bye to Gigi and headed out the door. Aly bumped into someone coming down the narrow hallway. She heard something fall to the floor.

"Whoops! Sorry," Aly said. She looked up to see Brandon and smiled. "Hey, we've got to stop meeting like this."

"Sorry," Brandon muttered. He reached into his shirt pocket, as though he had lost something.

Aly spotted what looked like a pack of gum on the floor. She reached down to pick it up. "I think you dropped this," she said, handing it to him. Then she stopped. The package of gum was Bubble Blast's Lime Invasion!

"Good flavor," Aly said quickly, trying to cover up her surprise.

"Yeah, thanks," Brandon said. He stuck the gum in his pocket and hurried past them.

Aly and AJ stared at each other in shock for a moment.

"Lime Invasion," Aly said.

"Did Brandon steal Gigi's equipment?" AJ

wondered. "But why would he do that? We've got to talk to him!"

They ran outside—and right into Jim.

"Glad to see you two are on time," Jim said, smiling. "You've got your first magazine interview across town."

AJ watched helplessly as Brandon disappeared around the corner. But there was nothing they could do.

New York City was waiting for them!

CHAPTER FIFTEEN:
A MUSICAL MOTIVE

Knock. Knock. Knock. Knock.

Aly lifted her head from her pillow. Morning sun streamed in through the hotel window. Their afternoon of interviews had spilled over into late evening. Both sisters were exhausted. It felt like they'd been to every single street in Manhattan.

AJ stumbled out of bed and opened the door. A man in a white uniform stood there, carrying a tray filled with covered plates.

"Room service," he said.

"Thanks," AJ told him. "Can you please put it on that table?"

The man set the tray on the table, and AJ signed the receipt he gave her and thanked him. Aly dragged herself out of bed and sat down next to Aly. There was a copy of *New York Weekend* magazine on the tray, topped with a note written on fancy white paper. AJ picked it up and read it.

"Girls, eat a good breakfast! Tonight's the big night! Love, Mom. P.S. The cover looks great!"

"Wow, today's Friday," Aly realized. "The first night of our tour. If I wasn't so tired, I'd be nervous."

AJ picked up the magazine and held it up so AJ could see the cover. She and her sister were draped over one of the carousel horses, smiling.

"Hey, that came out cute," AJ remarked.

The sisters slowly woke up as they dug into a fresh breakfast of fruit, French toast, eggs, and tall glasses of orange juice.

"I keep thinking of Brandon and that Lime Invasion gum," Aly said. "That makes him a suspect. But I can't think why he would steal Gigi's equipment."

"I know," AJ agreed. "Melanie has a motive. She thought Gigi stole all of the students for her school. And Miles needed money to record a CD. But why would Brandon do it?"

"It doesn't make sense," Aly added. "Brandon doesn't even like loud music. What would he want with a bunch of electric guitars and amps?"

AJ froze. She dropped her fork on her plate. Then the same thought hit Aly.

"That's his motive!" they both said at once.

"It all makes sense," AJ said. "Brandon complained about the noise from Gigi's school. They didn't want it to disturb their practice."

"That's why they left the acoustic guitars," Aly realized. "They're a lot quieter than electric guitars and amps."

She jumped out of her seat, then suddenly sat

back down. "Wait one second. Brandon doesn't look anything like Gigi. I don't think he could have fooled Mr. Willis."

AJ frowned. "You're right." She was thoughtful for a moment. "But he might have had help. Remember those other kids he was with at the park?"

"You mean Victor, that big guy who played the violin? How could he have passed for Gigi?" Aly asked.

AJ shook her head. "No, remember the girl with them? Her name was Christy, I think. She's about the same height as Gigi. And she has dark hair."

"That's got to be it!" Aly said, excited. "And I bet Victor helped carry out all that heavy equipment. Wow, I really feel like a detective now."

"We'd better tell Gigi right away," AJ said. "She's probably already talked to Melanie by now. I wonder if she called the police?"

Then AJ glanced at the note from their mom. A guilty look crossed her face. "I forgot. We can't go. We've got to start getting ready for the show tonight."

But Aly was already pulling on a pair of jeans. "It won't take long! We've got to do it. Come on, AJ!"

Minutes later, they were dressed and rushing out of the hotel lobby. To their amazement, Murray the cab driver was parked in front of the hotel.

"I was hoping to see you girls," he said, as they climbed in back. "Your manager was so nice. He got Sarah and me tickets for your show tonight. She's so excited! How can I ever thank you?"

"You can get us to the Girls Rock Academy, fast!" Aly replied.

CHAPTER SIXTEEN:
HARMONY

They reached the school in a few minutes, slightly nauseated, their hair tangled from the breeze blowing through the open cab windows.

"Was that fast enough for you?" Murray asked.

"That was awesome," Aly said.

"We'll see you and Sarah tonight," AJ said. "Thanks!"

They ran into the building and were faced with a puzzling sight. Gigi stood in the hallway, surrounded by electric guitars, amps, and soundboards. At first, AJ thought it was the equipment they had loaned Gigi. But nothing looked familiar.

"Gigi, what's going on?" AJ asked.

"I have no idea," Gigi said. "I walked in a few minutes ago, and all my stuff was here."

"Did you talk to Melanie yesterday? Maybe she brought it back," Aly suggested.

But Gigi shook her head. "I went to her school, but she wasn't there. So I left a note, asking her to meet me here today. Maybe she knew I was suspicious of her."

"Suspicious of what?"

Melanie walked through the door. "I got your note," she continued. "What did you want to talk to me about? And why are you suspicious?"

"Because I'm pretty sure you stole my equipment," Gigi blurted out. "Aly and AJ saw you selling one of my guitars at Izzy's shop. The red Gibson SG Special."

Melanie's eyes widened behind her glasses. AJ quickly jumped in.

"You've got it wrong, Gigi," she said quickly. "Aly and I know—"

"Why would I steal your equipment?" Melanie interrupted, her voice rising. "That's the craziest thing I've ever heard!"

"Then what were you doing selling my guitar?" Gigi yelled back.

"You mean that one?" Melanie asked, pointing to the pile of equipment.

Gigi looked, then got suddenly quiet. She walked over and picked up a cherry red Gibson SG Special.

"Uh, yeah, this one," she said sheepishly.

"That guitar I sold was mine," Melanie said. "I sank all my money into my school, but I have no students. I have to pay the bills somehow."

"Wait," Gigi said, sighing heavily. "I don't get it. What is going on here?"

"That's what we're trying to tell you—" Aly began, but there was another interruption. Brandon,

Christy, and Victor came down the hall, carrying their instrument cases.

"Hey, guys," Gigi said absently.

"Are you going somewhere?" Aly asked curiously.

"We're going to find a new practice space," Brandon said sullenly. "We can't practice here anymore. Not with lots of loud guitar playing going on."

AJ stepped forward. "That's why you stole Gigi's guitars, isn't it?" she said, looking Brandon in the eyes. "You were hoping she'd close her school, and you'd still have your practice space."

Gigi gasped, and Brandon looked away. Victor was blushing, and Christy looked like she wanted to melt into the floor.

"Look, we're sorry," Brandon said finally. "It's so hard to find affordable practice space in this city. The rooms upstairs are perfect, and the acoustics are great."

"So you were going to ruin my business because of great acoustics?" Gigi asked angrily.

Christy Sung's face was bright red. "We feel terrible!" she blurted out. "That's why we returned the equipment."

"Yes, it was not a nice thing to do," Victor added.

"We're really sorry," Brandon said, and he sounded genuine. "And we're leaving the building, so you won't ever have to see us again."

"You know, a little ceiling insulation might just solve the problem."

AJ and Aly turned, surprised, at the sound of Jim's voice. He smiled.

"I came to get our equipment back," he said. "I couldn't help hearing everything. It wouldn't take much to insulate your rooms, Gigi. That would keep the sound of your students down here, where it belongs."

Gigi didn't look happy. But she considered Jim's idea. "I guess I could do that."

"Why would you even want us to stay?" Christy wailed. "We did a terrible thing to you."

"Well, you did give me my stuff back," Gigi said.

"And we're all musicians, after all. We've got to look out for one another, right? So I might as well forgive you."

"You will not regret it," Victor said.

"Yeah," Brandon added. "We'll make it up to you somehow."

"You won't even know we're here," Christy said.

"Maybe we can all do better than that," AJ said. She gave Aly a look—a look that Aly immediately understood. They walked into Gigi's classroom. Puzzled, everyone followed.

"Aly and I hardly ever fight, but when we do, playing together always makes things better," AJ said, strapping on an acoustic guitar.

"It helps brings the harmony back to our relationship," Aly added. She'd picked up a guitar, too, and now she was tuning it.

AJ began to play a series of notes. "That song you guys were playing in Central Park the other day was beautiful," she said. "It went something like this, didn't it?"

Victor was the first to get the idea. "Ah, yes, yes.

That's very close." He quickly opened up his violin case and took a seat. Soon he was playing along with AJ.

Aly improvised, adding some chords and a funky little beat to the classical tune. Christy shyly took out her violin and began to play.

Melanie grinned, shaking her head. "That's pretty cool," she said. She turned to Gigi. "Okay if I grab a guitar?"

Gigi nodded, and Melanie quickly joined the jam. That left Jim standing against the wall, grinning, and Gigi and Brandon looking warily at each other.

"Might as well," she said finally. She smiled at Brandon. "How about it?"

Brandon smiled back, looking relieved. "Sure," he said.

They all played together for a few minutes, until Jim interrupted them.

"I hate to do this, but I've got to get Aly and AJ and our equipment out of here," he said. "We've got to get ready for tonight's show."

Everyone stopped playing. Aly looked at Jim with pleading eyes. "Speaking of the show, do you think—"

Jim reached into his pocket and took out some tickets. "As generous as you two are, I've always got extra tickets on hand. Here you go, guys. Front row seats. Don't be late."

Christy took her ticket with shining eyes. "Wow, thanks." Brandon took his a little reluctantly. Aly grinned at him.

"Better bring your earplugs, Brandon," she said. "It might get a little loud!"

La la la la la la . . .

CHAPTER SEVENTEEN:
DETECTIVES *AND* MUSICIANS

"Hello, New York!" AJ yelled from the stage of Madison Square Garden.

This time, thousands of screaming fans answered her. She looked at Aly and smiled.

"Aly and I want to welcome you to the very first stop on our tour," she said into the mic. "We're totally psyched to be here."

"We met a lot of great people here in New York!" Aly added.

Another cheer went up. The girls had been stricken with the jitters just a few moments ago, but those feelings evaporated as soon as they got on stage. That's when adrenaline took over, the rush of the stage, the roar of the crowd. They had their band behind them, their fans in front of them, and there was no better feeling than that.

AJ nodded to the band, and they launched into "Potential Breakup Song." The crowd went wild at the sound of the hit song.

"La la la la . . ."

Both sisters smiled as they sang. The bright stage lights were nearly blinding, but they could make out a few familiar faces in the front row. Gigi and Melanie were sitting next to each other, rocking to the music. Brandon, Christy, and Victor sat nearby. Toward stage right, Aly thought she saw Murray with a little girl.

The show went off without any problems. The sisters did their whole set, then came back for an encore. When they finally left the stage for the last time, they were a little sweaty, but full of energy.

"What a wonderful show!" Carrie said, squeezing them both in a big hug. "I'm so proud of you."

"It was great," Jim said, beaming. "Now let me get you back to your dressing room."

Jim ushered them through the maze behind the stage to their dressing room, where cold bottles of water, a fruit platter, and a bowl of Aly's favorite candy waited for them. They both flopped down on the couch there and slammed a bottle of water each.

"I'll go manage the crowds outside," Jim said, leaving them alone for a moment. It felt strange to be in a room with just the two of them, after they'd just left a space full of thousands of people.

"That was amazing!" Aly said, a little loudly. Standing near the big speakers on stage made their ears a little fuzzy after a show sometimes.

"It was a great start," AJ said. "I can't wait for the rest of the tour."

Jim opened the door a crack. "Feel like seeing some fans?"

"Sure!" both girls answered.

Gigi and Melanie entered the room together.

"That was an awesome show," Gigi said.

"Totally," Melanie said. "We just wanted to say thanks for the tickets."

"And thanks for pointing out how silly we were acting," Gigi said. "We acted like enemies, but we have so much in common. We like the same music, and even have the same guitars."

Melanie looked really happy. "Gigi's invited me to teach at the school with her. So I get to see my dream come true after all."

"That's so great!" AJ said, hugging them both. "That's a perfect solution."

Shannon and Hana came into the dressing room next, followed by Shannon's dad and Hana's mom.

"We wanted to thank you for bringing the girls together," Shannon's dad said.

"I've never seen Hana so happy," Hana's mom added.

The two girls stepped forward.

"We're going to name our guitars, just like you do," Shannon said.

Hana smiled. "And we thought of the best names. I'm going to name mine Aly, and Shannon's going to name hers AJ!"

"Ooh, you girls are so cute!" Aly cried. She grabbed a camera from the dressing room table. "We have got to get a picture. Come on!"

Aly and AJ took a picture with Shannon and Hana. Gigi and Melanie wanted pictures, too.

"I owe you guys big-time," Gigi told them. "If you ever come back to New York, I'll give you a personal tour. I think you were too busy helping me out to do anything fun. You two are like detectives, solving the mystery like that."

"I guess you could say we're musicians *and* detectives," AJ said, grinning at her sister.

"Or detective musicians," Aly answered. "I kind of like the sound of that."

"Anyway, I think we got a real feel for New York," AJ added. "We met a lot of people—"

"—and we ate bagels and real New York pizza," Aly said. "And don't forget Central Park, and the shopping . . ."

Jim poked his head into the dressing room. "Your mom says to tell you not to stay up too late tonight. We're heading to Miami in the morning."

"Do you need a ride to the airport?"

Murray the cab driver pushed his way into the dressing room, holding the hand of his young granddaughter. Aly and AJ looked at each other, then burst out laughing.

"No, thanks, Murray," AJ said.

Aly grinned. "We want to make it to Miami in one piece!"